Library of Congress Cataloging in Publication Data:
Cosgrove, Stephen. Cranky. (A Whimsie storybook) SUMMARY: Switch Witch takes advantage of Moonbeam's desire to stay up past his bedtime by giving him a Magic Light that keeps him awake and makes him cranky 1. Children's stories, American. [1. Sleep—Fiction. 2. Bedtime—Fiction. 3. Witches—Fiction] I. Reasoner, Charles, ill. II. Title. III. Series: Cosgrove, Stephen. Whimsie storybook. PZ7.C8187Cp 1985   [E]   85-42712   ISBN: 0-394-87454-4

Manufactured in Belgium
1   2   3   4   5   6   7   8   9   0

Cranky

by Stephen Cosgrove

illustrated by Charles Reasoner

Random House New York

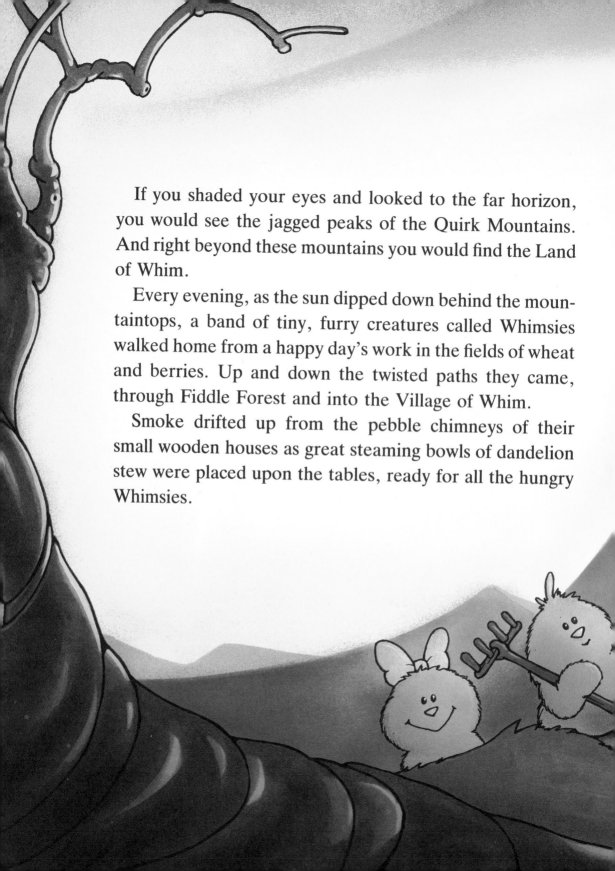

If you shaded your eyes and looked to the far horizon, you would see the jagged peaks of the Quirk Mountains. And right beyond these mountains you would find the Land of Whim.

Every evening, as the sun dipped down behind the mountaintops, a band of tiny, furry creatures called Whimsies walked home from a happy day's work in the fields of wheat and berries. Up and down the twisted paths they came, through Fiddle Forest and into the Village of Whim.

Smoke drifted up from the pebble chimneys of their small wooden houses as great steaming bowls of dandelion stew were placed upon the tables, ready for all the hungry Whimsies.

At the end of the day, right after supper, all the grown-up Whimsies would gather at the center of the village. There they would build a fire of juniper and sage and sit around it telling gentle tales of wonder and awe—tales about Whimsies of the past and their gentle ways. They would sit as the smoke filled the air with the essence of burning spices.

Poor little Moonbeam, the very youngest Whimsie, wished he could stay up with all the grown-ups at the campfire, but he needed his rest and was sent to bed just as soon as the fireflies sparked at the moon.

Every night, after his parents had gone to meet the other Whimsies, Moonbeam would stand on his tippy toes and peek out the window at all the festivities.

"Why do I always have to miss out on all the fun?" Moonbeam complained to himself.

But after watching for a while, Moonbeam would always get sleepy. Then he would slide between the cool sheets, pull his warm quilt right up to his nose, and fall into a deep sleep.

One night, after Moonbeam had fallen asleep, he was awakened by a soft croaking voice which kept calling, "Moonbeam, Moonbeam."

"Who is that?" said Moonbeam, yawning as he rubbed the sleep from his eyes. There, looking in the window, was a very old woman. She was holding a golden lamp which

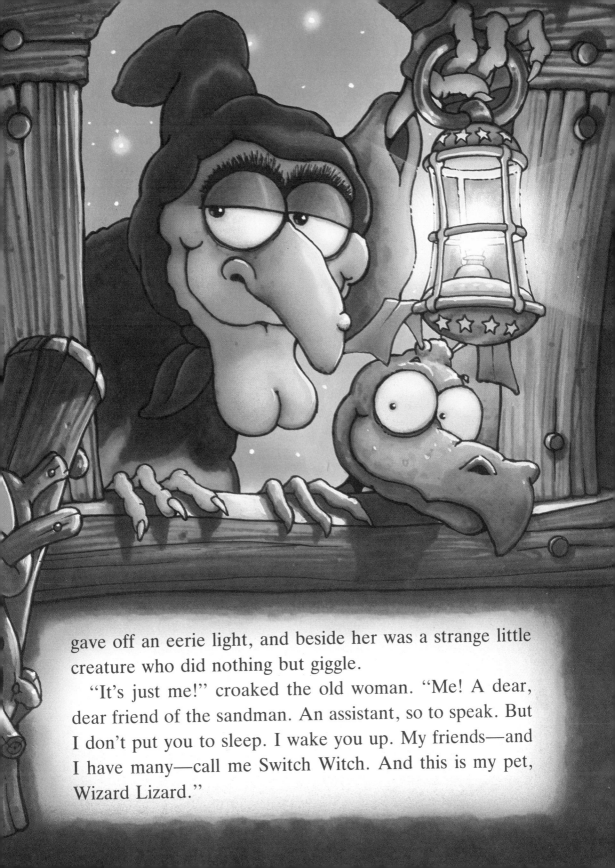

gave off an eerie light, and beside her was a strange little creature who did nothing but giggle.

"It's just me!" croaked the old woman. "Me! A dear, dear friend of the sandman. An assistant, so to speak. But I don't put you to sleep. I wake you up. My friends—and I have many—call me Switch Witch. And this is my pet, Wizard Lizard."

"What do you want?" Moonbeam asked nervously.

"Want?" asked Switch Witch. "I want nothing, but I have brought you a magical gift." With that she handed the Whimsie the golden lamp. "This is the Magic Light. As long as it is lit you can stay awake as long as you like." Switch Witch and Wizard Lizard then disappeared in a swirl of giggles and laughter.

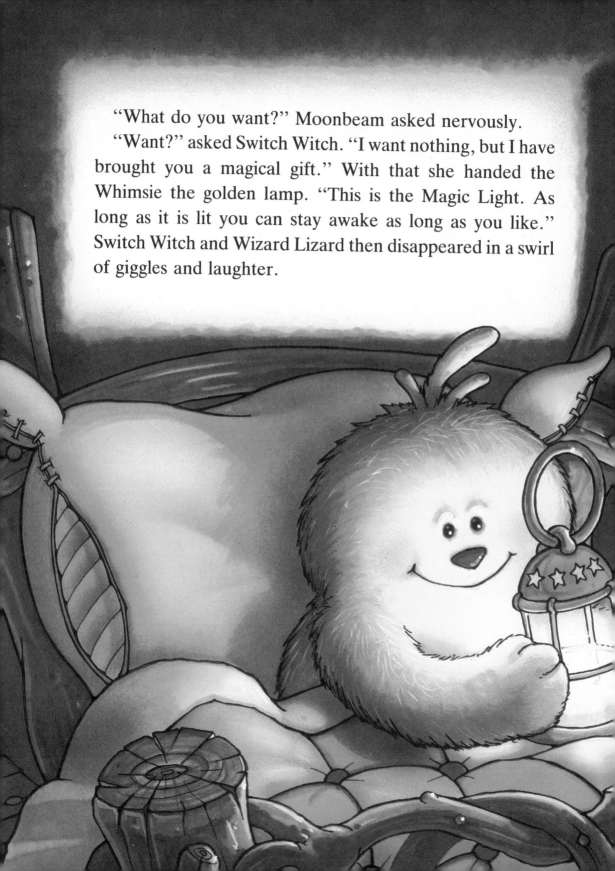

With the Magic Light, Moonbeam didn't feel the least bit tired. He set the magic lamp on the floor and pulled out his favorite toys from beneath his bed.

All night long he played with his favorite toys—Noah's Ark with all the animals, a spinning top, and a turtle named Tom.

When morning came and the sun began to peek through the open window, Moonbeam hid the magic lamp beneath his bed and rushed out of his room to greet the day.

That morning all the Whimsies in Moonbeam's family happily helped put breakfast on the table. They whistled gay little tunes as great bowls of bundle berries and stacks of roasted toast smothered in dandelion jam were placed on the table.

Moonbeam didn't say good morning to anybody. He sat down with a thump and shoved his breakfast aside. "I hate

bundle berries! I hate dandelion jam! And I hate roast toast most!'' Moonbeam announced to his family.

"Why, Moonbeam, what's gotten into you?'' asked his mother. "Are you feeling all right?'' And she felt his furry brow to see if he was sick.

"I'm fine!'' shouted Moonbeam. "I'm just not hungry.''

"Well, you sure are cranky,'' said his father.

All day long Moonbeam got crankier and crankier. That night as usual Moonbeam was sent to bed while the older Whimsies stayed up around the fire. No sooner had his mother left his room than out came the magic lamp, and right away he didn't feel tired anymore. He got out his toys and started to play.

Later, much later, when all the other Whimsies were fast asleep, Moonbeam sneaked out into the fields of clover. With the Magic Light glowing softly and keeping him awake, he looked up at all the wondrous stars. And when the first rays of the morning sun came peeking across the Quirk Mountains, he was still awake.

Like a shadow he slipped back into his room and hid the lamp again. Then he pretended to wake up with the rest of his family.

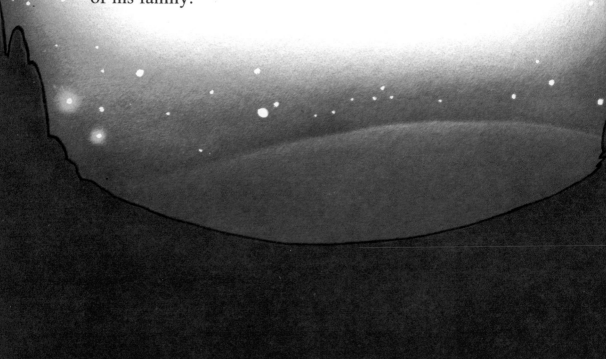

Later that day Moonbeam's sister rushed up to him and said, "Look at the pretty blue ribbon in my hair."

"I hate ribbons, I hate blue, and most of all I don't like you!" snapped Moonbeam. With that he yanked the ribbon and stormed down the street, leaving his sister in tears. Without any sleep for two nights Moonbeam was really cranky now.

Up and down the street he stormed, kicking cans and bumping into anything that got in his way. "Isn't that Moonbeam?" asked one Whimsie.

"Not anymore," said another. "Moonbeam's become a cranky monster!"

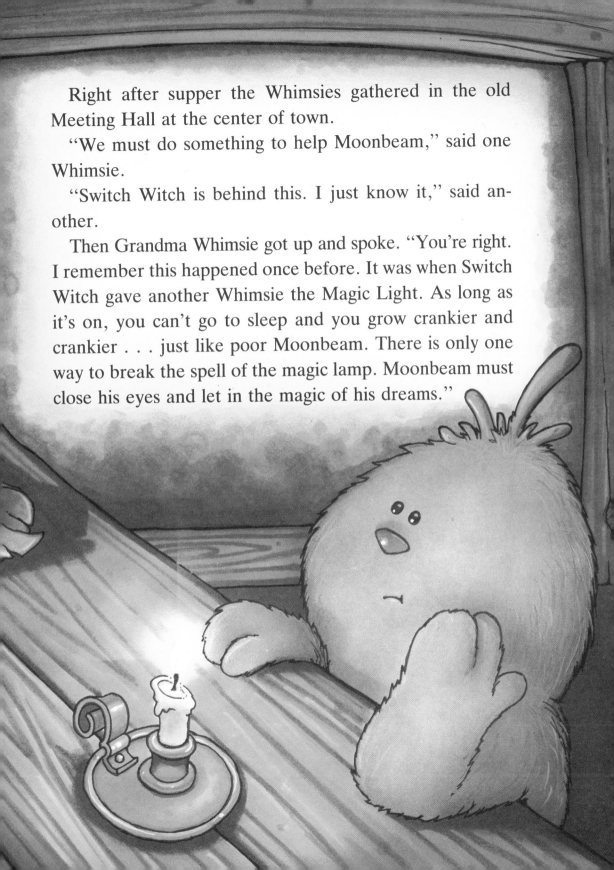

Right after supper the Whimsies gathered in the old Meeting Hall at the center of town.

"We must do something to help Moonbeam," said one Whimsie.

"Switch Witch is behind this. I just know it," said another.

Then Grandma Whimsie got up and spoke. "You're right. I remember this happened once before. It was when Switch Witch gave another Whimsie the Magic Light. As long as it's on, you can't go to sleep and you grow crankier and crankier . . . just like poor Moonbeam. There is only one way to break the spell of the magic lamp. Moonbeam must close his eyes and let in the magic of his dreams."

Quickly Grandma Whimsie led all the other Whimsies to Moonbeam's house, where they gathered outside his window. In rhythm to a cricket's tune they began to sing a whimsical Whimsie lullaby. They sang and they sang, but just when they felt that Moonbeam must be fast asleep, he popped his head up in the window and shouted, "Go away! With all your stupid singing I can't play."

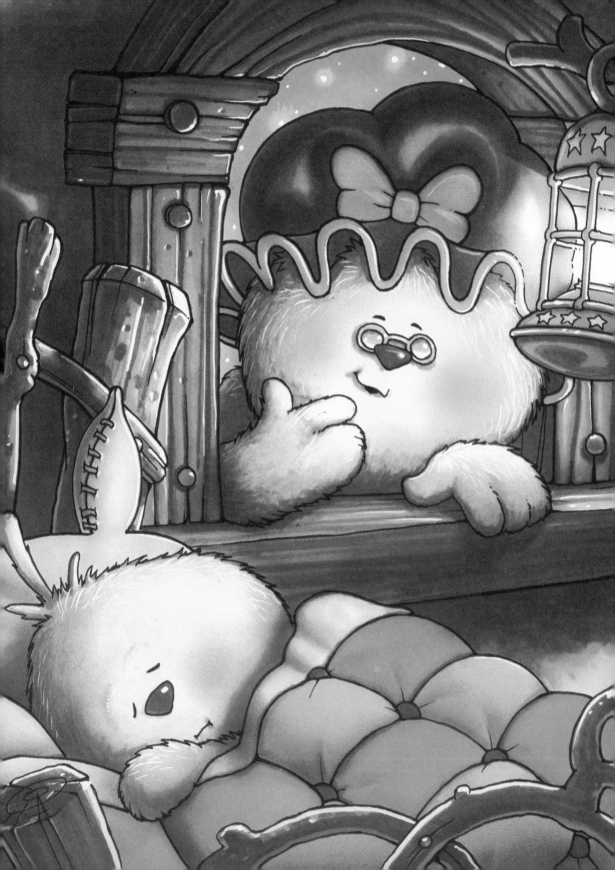

"Moonbeam, aren't you tired?" asked Grandma Whimsie in a soft and gentle voice.

"If you want me to go to sleep, you can forget it," said Moonbeam as he lay on his bed reading a book. "I'm awake and I'm not going to miss any fun by being asleep!"

The old Whimsie continued softly, "Ahh, but you are missing something."

"What?" Moonbeam growled.

"The game of dreams," said the old Whimsie.

"What's that?" he asked.

"Listen and do as I say," said Grandma Whimsie. "Close your eyes and see in your mind the River Whim as it flows gently by. Build a raft of tule weeds and float down the river, bobbing in the gentle current."

Moonbeam yawned. "I do feel very tired. Maybe I'll just rest my eyes for a minute."

Grandma Whimsie smiled. "Moonbeam?" she called gently. "Moonbeam?"

There was no answer, for the littlest Whimsie had fallen asleep.

In the shadow of starlight the Whimsies slipped into Moonbeam's room and covered the Magic Light with an old quilt. Poof! Just like that, the lamp disappeared and went back to its original owner.

Outside, in the darkened night, Switch Witch and Wizard Lizard could be seen sitting with eyes opened wide because they couldn't go to sleep in the glare of the Magic Light.

One by one the lights went out in the Whimsie village, and dreams began to swirl in the gentle breeze that blew. Everyone, even Moonbeam himself, knew that he would wake in the morning his usual cheerful self.

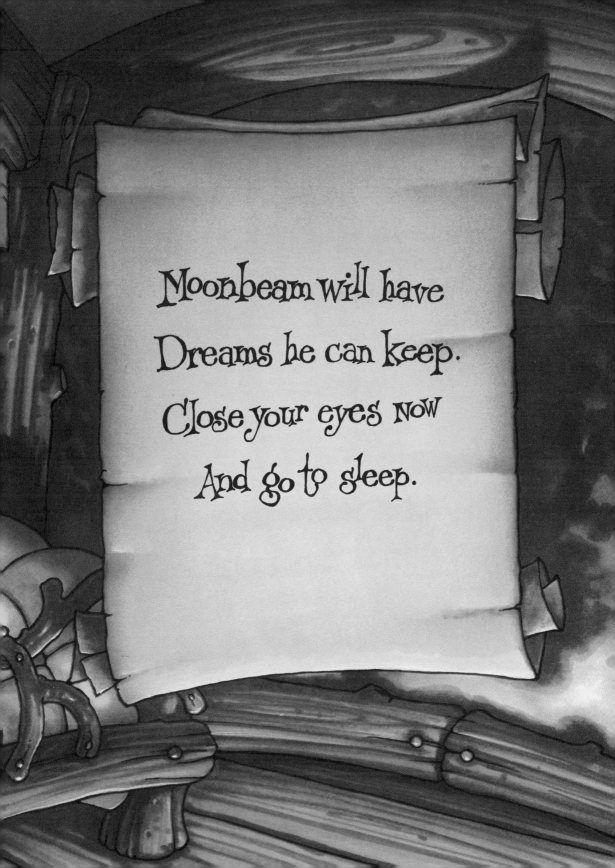

Moonbeam will have
Dreams he can keep.
Close your eyes now
And go to sleep.